Let's Play Tag!

📖 Read the Page

▶ Read the Story

★ Game

😊 Yes   ☹ No

🔄 Repeat

⬛ Stop

💻

THE PRINCESS AND THE FROG

Tiana's New Dream

Once upon a time, a girl named Tiana lived in New Orleans. Tiana dreamed that one day she would own her own restaurant. She knew that the only way to make her dream come true was through hard work. So Tiana worked very hard.

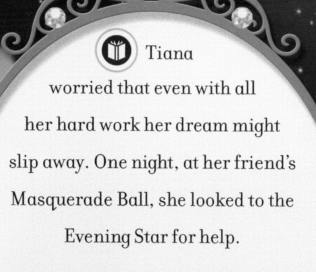 Tiana worried that even with all her hard work her dream might slip away. One night, at her friend's Masquerade Ball, she looked to the Evening Star for help.

"Fairy tales say a wish upon the Evening Star is sure to come true. *Please, please, please,*" she wished, "help me get my restaurant."

But instead, Tiana's wish granted her a frog!

"I am Prince Naveen," said the frog. Seeing Tiana in her lovely gown and tiara, he thought she was a princess.

"You must kiss me!" he said. "Then I will turn back into a charming and handsome prince."

"Look, I'd like to help you," said Tiana, "but I just do not kiss frogs."

"Oh, but you must kiss me," replied the frog. "I happen to come from a fabulously wealthy family. Surely I could offer you some type of reward ... a wish I could grant?"

Tiana reconsidered the frog's request. Maybe they could help one another. If her kiss broke the spell the prince would give her a reward and she could get her restaurant.

"Okay, Tiana, you can do this!" she tried to convince herself. She gathered up her courage, puckered up, and ... **smooch!**

poof!

But since Tiana wasn't a real princess, her kiss didn't break the spell. Instead it made it worse.

When she opened her eyes, not only was the prince still a frog, now she was one too!

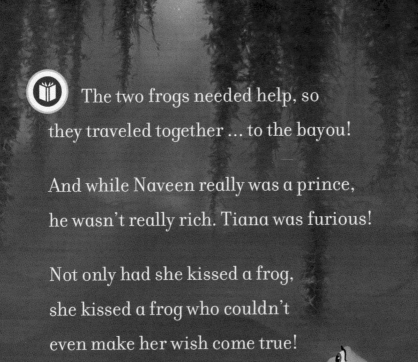

The two frogs needed help, so
they traveled together ... to the bayou!

And while Naveen really was a prince,
he wasn't really rich. Tiana was furious!

Not only had she kissed a frog,
she kissed a frog who couldn't
even make her wish come true!

Naveen was just as
angry. He thought Tiana was
a princess whose kiss would break
the spell. Instead, she was just a girl
dressed up like a princess for a party.

It looked like neither of their
dreams was going to
come true.

In the bayou, the two frogs met Louis the alligator and Ray the firefly.

Tiana and Naveen's new friends offered to help the frogs find a way to break the spell and turn them back into humans.

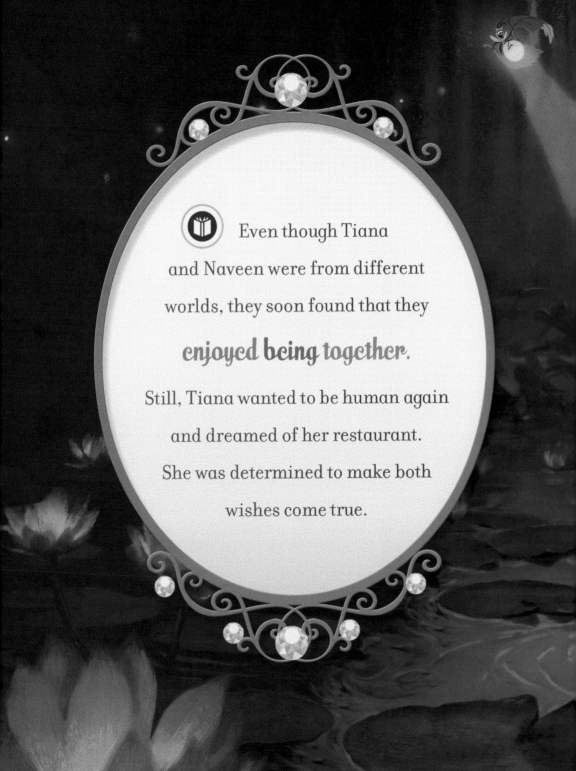

Even though Tiana and Naveen were from different worlds, they soon found that they **enjoyed being together**. Still, Tiana wanted to be human again and dreamed of her restaurant. She was determined to make both wishes come true.

As their adventure took them from the bayou back to New Orleans for Mardi Gras …

… **they fell in love.**

Now, they each had a new dream, one they shared together.

Back in the bayou,
Tiana and Naveen's new dream came
true when they were married ... as frogs.

And when they kissed,

another dream came true. They became
human! Naveen was stunned.
"Once you became my wife ...
that made you ..."

"A princess. You just kissed yourself a princess!" said Tiana.

The spell was finally broken!

Now that they had become human, Tiana and Naveen went back to New Orleans and had a royal wedding.

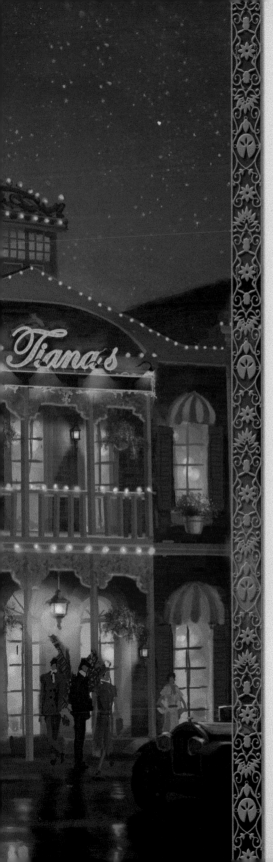

Princess Tiana and
Prince Naveen opened
Tiana's restaurant.

They lived happily ever
after ... because together,

all their dreams came true!